AF538371

To Mrs. Stradley,
Merry Christmas — 2002
Melissa Bourbon Ramirez
Sam Ramirez

# the flight of the sunflower

Melissa Bourbon Ramirez

illustrated by Nadine Takvorian

**All About Kids Publishing**
**6280 San Ignacio Avenue, Suite C**
**San Jose, CA 95119**

Book Design by Shanti Nelson Design

*Printed in Hong Kong*



**All About Kids Publishing**
**6280 San Ignacio Avenue, Suite C**
**San Jose, CA 95119**

Library of Congress catalog card number: 00-103956
ISBN 0-9700863-0-X

For Mom and Dad who encouraged me to find my own place in the world where I could take root and thrive.
-M.B.R.

For Grandma, Grandpa, Nona,
and Hratch deh-deh
-N.T.

A golden sunflower stood tall and radiant, basking in the sunlight. It held its head high and stood firmly planted in the soil. It was content with its beautiful home and miraculous life.

A gentle breeze blew through the quiet field where the flower lived. The sunflower swayed back and forth, dancing in the wind. Gentle though it was, the force of the breeze was enough to dislodge a tiny seedling from the face of the golden flower, sending it hurling through the air. "Ah!" yelped the seedling, tumbling and rolling in the wind's current.

"Do not be frightened little seed. I am your friend. Come with me.
Let me show you the world," the wind whistled.

"But you are taking me from my home," the seed cried, looking down at its mother rooted in the ground. Her golden face seemed to follow the young seedling as it sailed through the air.

The wind whistled and gently explained, "You are meant to grow little seed. You must make a home of your own. I will show you the beauty that lives all around you and then you may choose your home."

The seedling did not know about the Earth's vast beauty. It had only lived with its mother in a safe and protected world. "I want to go home," it said again. But the wind did not listen. It carried the seed high over the land, swirling like a tornado, zooming above the trees.

As the seedling and the wind began their journey, they passed over a velvety, green field. The tiny seed saw the beautiful landscape below and cheered up. "Oh! It is wonderful! How I'd love to plant my roots here!" the seedling exclaimed.

But, the wind did not listen and replied, "You have not seen anything yet little friend. Be patient." It continued carrying the seedling high above the ground, leaving the velvety field behind.

The seed gazed upon the Earth as he soared overhead. In the distance the seedling spotted a dazzling garden full of bright, colorful flowers. "Oh! That's where I want to live," the seed said excitedly. The breeze continued blowing. "Please, powerful wind, put me down in that lovely garden!" the sunflower seed pleaded.

But, the wind did not listen. It raced along, carrying the seed with it. From below, orange poppies, lavender snapdragons and white daisies waved at the young seed as it passed by.

Disappointed at leaving the beautiful garden behind, the seedling nearly missed seeing the grace of the vast desert looming in the distance. "Look at the elegance of the desert little one," the wind pointed out. "It is so simple, yet so lovely."

They approached a vast area of sand dunes and the seedling was speechless. It stared at the rolling hills of sand, taking in its delights. Tiny granules of sand zoomed by, racing with the wind. The seedling watched them somersault through the air. A few tiny granules of sand slowed and joined the sunflower seed. "Where are you going?" the granules asked.

"I am learning about the world," the seed replied. "A gentle breeze came along and shook me from my home. My mother, a golden sunflower, stood brave and tall resisting the powerful wind. But I am just a small seedling. I could not withstand the force of the wind, so it carried me with it to see the world." The sand and the young seedling tumbled through the air, looping around one another.

"We have an idea!" the sand exclaimed together. "Why don't you come join us in the desert? It is a warm, sunny place to live. You can stay with us there."

The sunflower seed trembled, overjoyed by the invitation, but realized that it could not thrive in the desert. "I would love to live with you in the desert, but it is not possible," it replied, disappointedly.

"Why?" the sand asked, puzzled.

"A seed must have water to grow and thrive. There is little water in the desert. I could not survive there."

"We understand," the sand said, "We can only be free where there is little water, since water holds us down and prevents us from soaring through the air." As the edge of the desert approached, the sand said good-bye to the seedling and returned to their desert home. The breeze continued blowing, carrying the seedling away from the warm desert and the friendly sand.

As the seed continued on its journey, it crossed over the powerful ocean. A seagull spotted the tiny fleck and flew beside it. "Where are you going?" the bird asked the seed. "I do not know," the seed replied, glad to make another friend. The seedling shared its story with its newest companion.

"Why don't I carry you on my wing and drop you down upon the sea?" the seagull asked. "It is a very remarkable place. You'll meet fascinating creatures living underwater. There you can swim and play and bask in the sun. The ocean can be your new home."

The sunflower seed gazed at the restless ocean. It wished he could ride the seagull's wing. The seedling sighed. "I cannot," he told the bird, sadly. I am just a tiny seed. I would blend in with the salt, the krill and the plankton, and a fish would come along and swallow me up. I want to grow and grow and become a golden sunflower. I need land and soil and fresh water." The seagull nodded its head in understanding and flew away. Alone, the seedling continued on its journey with the mighty wind.

Flying over the ocean's currents strengthened the wind's force. The tiny sunflower seed was quickly swept up into fluffy, white clouds. "Hello there!" the clouds bellowed, when they saw the seedling. "Have you come to join us in our lofty paradise?"

"I would love to stop in your lovely home, but I cannot," replied the seedling, as it sped past. I must go where there is land and water." The seed's words echoed, softly fading away as the wind carried it off on its journey. The clouds silently wished the seed luck and waved good-bye.

A gust of wind came up and swept the seed through the ocean air. Turning and spinning, together the seedling and wind soared swiftly back through the cloud's home and back over the sea. The tiny sunflower seed nodded hello to the seagull and the glorious water below as it passed by.

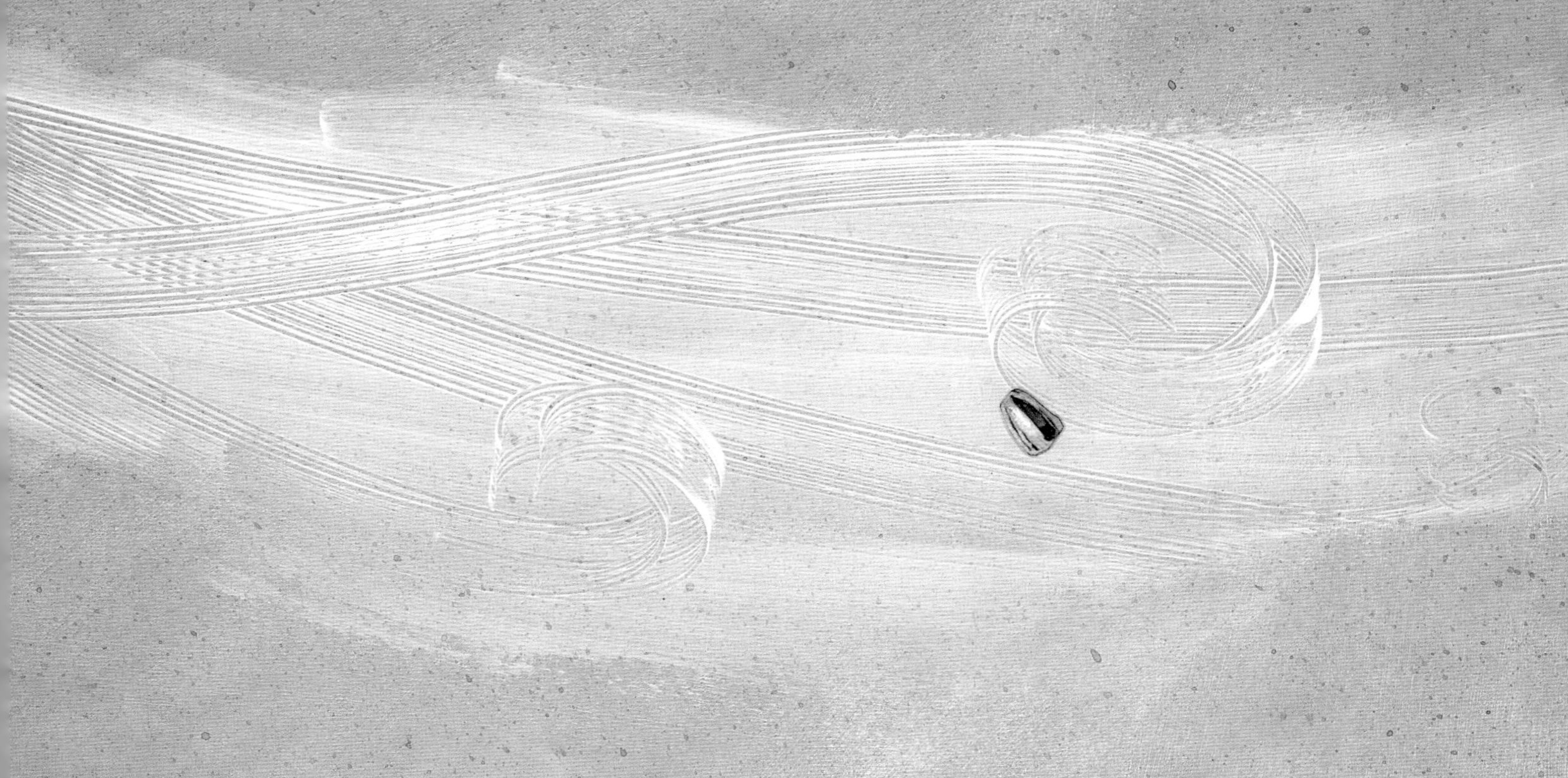

Together with the wind, the seed traveled back over the rolling desert. The sand rejoined the seed for a short while and then wished it well, waving good-bye one last time.

The wind slowed and gently passed back over the glorious flower garden and the lush, green field. As the tiny seedling flew over the land, taking in every aspect of its beauty, it longed for a place of its own. It knew that the field was not its home and the garden was already full of flowers. The seedling needed to find a home and make its own place in the world.

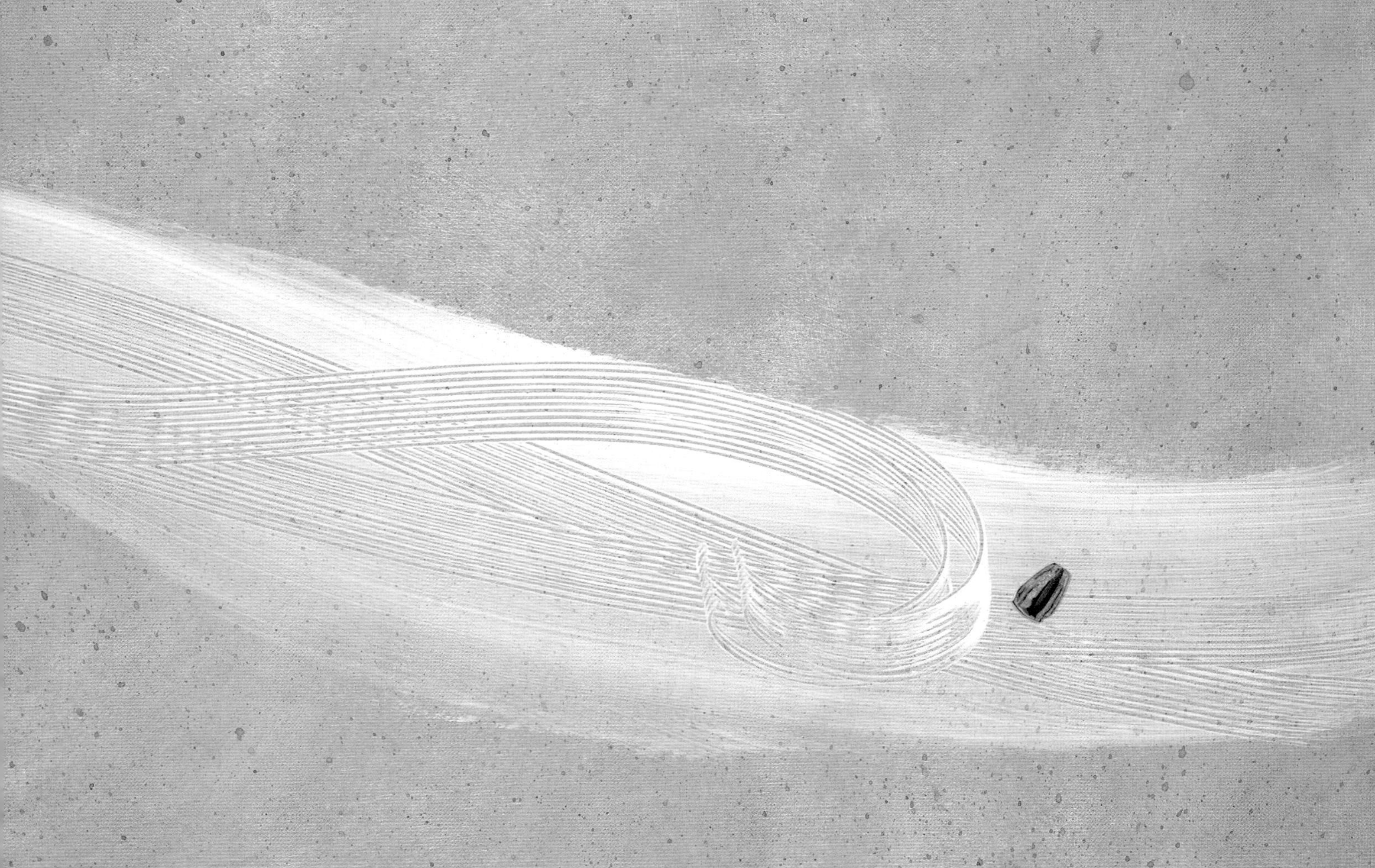

Finally, the wind's force began to fade and it asked, "Isn't the world a glorious place?" Exhausted at first, the sunflower seed perked up from the wind's excitement, renewing the seed's energy.

"It is! It is!" the seedling exclaimed, thinking of its adventures and all the things it had seen. It remembered the friendly sand and the thoughtful seagull and the welcoming clouds. The seedling's memories of the vibrant flowers, sharing their flowerbed and the lush field, flowing with green grass rushed back. "I wish I had a place to call my own, where I could grow and live and flourish as they all do," the seedling sighed.

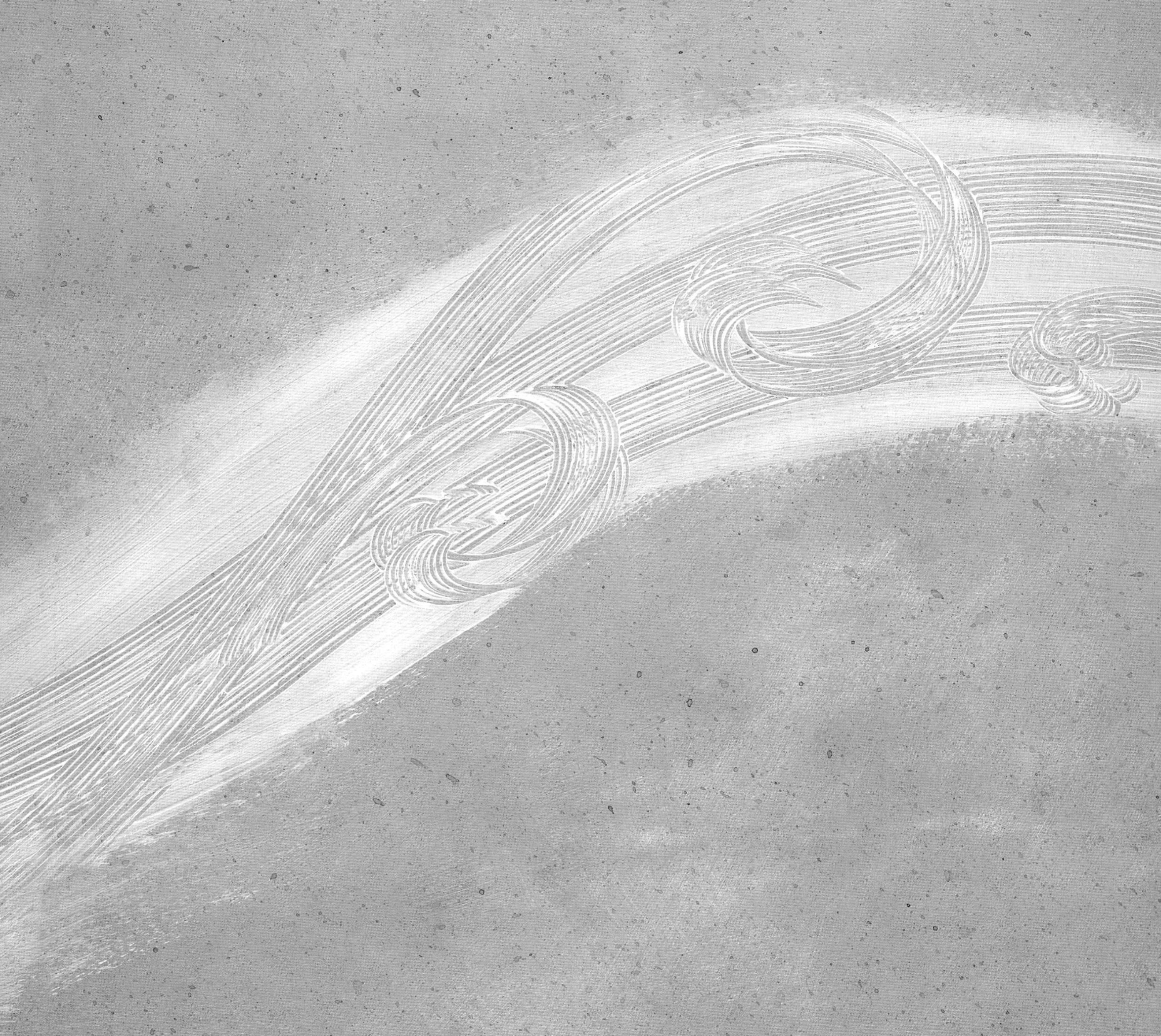

"Oh, but you do. You have only to choose it," the wind replied. "Where do you want your home to be?"

Thinking, the tiny sunflower seed gazed at the Earth below. It saw its mother, the golden sunflower, in the distance. There she stood, proud and tall and solidly rooted in the Earth. For a moment, the seedling longed to be with its mother, and feel the security of her golden face shading it. "I can not go there," the seedling said aloud. "It is time for me to find my own home."

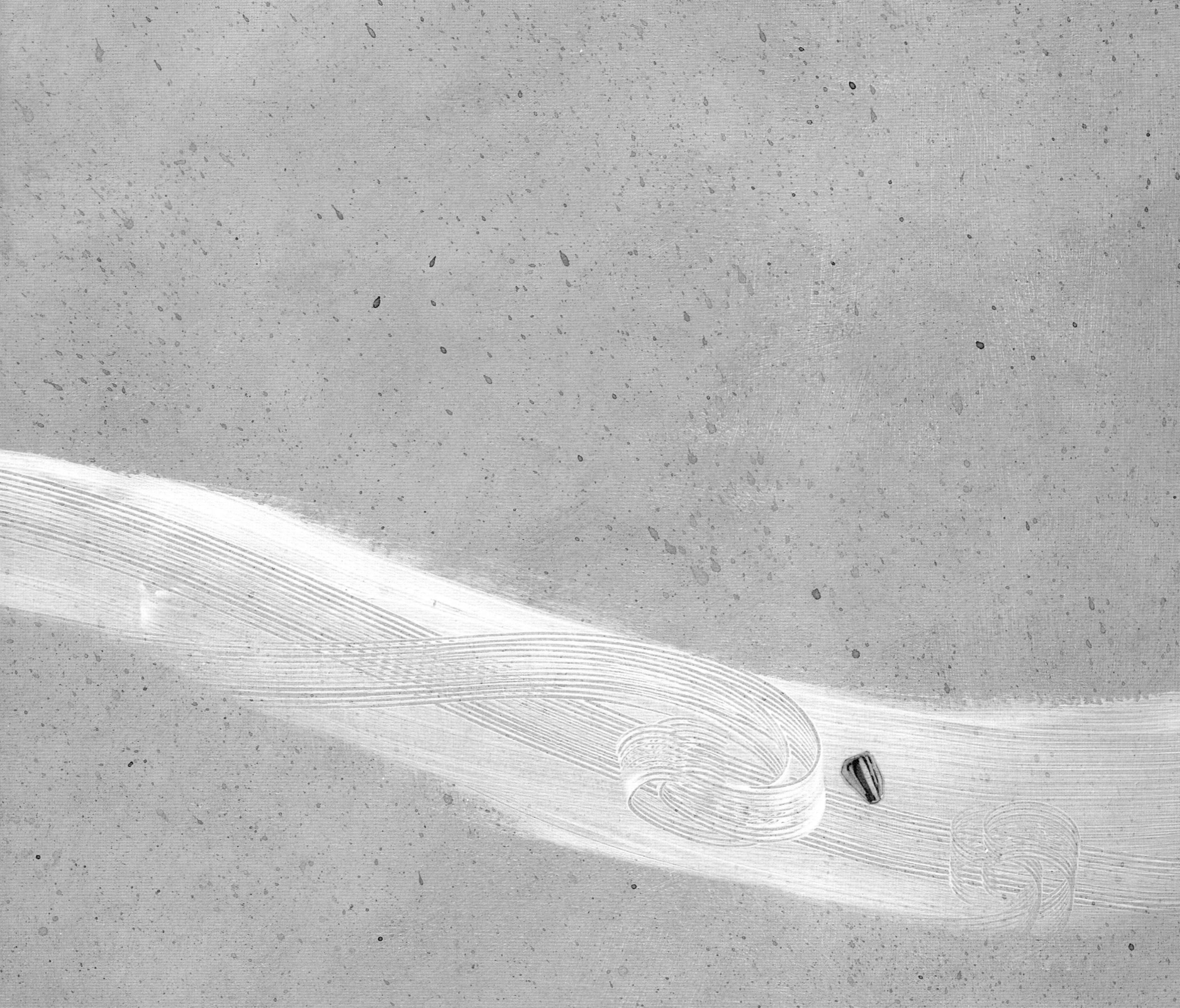

The wind whistled in agreement. "Home is wherever you want it to be. Where you are content and can grow strong, but you cannot live in your mother's shadow forever. She has given you her strength and her beauty and her power. Now you must take those things and learn to grow strong on your own. I have shown you the beauty of the world. Now I must go," the wind whispered. "I wish you well little seed."

The seed understood. "I must have fertile Earth, life-giving water and radiant sun. These things give me life and will provide me with a home," the seed said. "Then," it added, "I will grow into a golden sunflower. I talked with the clouds; they will bring me water to grow. I saw the field where the soil is rich. I learned about the desert where water is scarce, and traveled to the ocean where water covers the land——and I saw the beauty in each. And I viewed a garden, full of flowers. It is now my turn to find a home where I can plant myself firm in the ground. Down there, where the soil is rich, will be my home. Thank you, mighty wind."

The seedling looped out of the breeze and dropped to the fertile Earth below. Its mother stood nearby, a constant and reassuring force. The sunflower seedling knew this would be its new home.

The wind whistled a final good-bye and blew away. A cloud floated by overhead and a sprinkle of water touched the golden sunflower seed's face. It looked up and nodded thank you to its friend. The young sunflower seed burrowed into the moist, rich soil of its new home and began to take root. It smiled, content with its beautiful home and miraculous life.